A WARNING FROM THE BARON

Many travellers write books. Sad to say not all of these are as honest as myself. Some of them are careless with the truth. Some are given to harmless fables. But others publish volumes packed with frauds, fakes, false-hoods, fictions, fibs, clap-trap, moonshine, whoppers and terminological inexactitudes.

I flatter myself that my own life has been interesting enough. Do my books need tall stories? Does a fish need water? Do you reader doubt my word? You do? Well, name your weapon. I will meet you for a duel at the south gate of the Garden of Eden next February 31st.

Yours very faithfully,

Baron Munchausen

Text © 1987 Adrian Mitchell. Illustrations © 1987 Patrick Benson. First published in the United States of America in 1987 by Philomel Books, a division of The Putnam Publishing Group, 51 Madison Avenue, New York, NY 10010. First published in 1987 by Walker Books Ltd. 184-192 Drummond Street, London NW1 3HP. Printed and bound by L.E.G.O., Vicenza, Italy. All rights reserved. Library of Congress Cataloging-in-Publication Data Mitchell, Adrian, 1932-   The Baron all at sea. Summary: Baron Munchausen undertakes a perilous journey to aid a choir of 1000 Africans in returning home from a European concert. [1. Voyages and travels—Fiction.   2. Tall tales. 3. Humorous stories] I. Benson, Patrick, ill. II. Title.   PZ7.M685Bao   1987 [Fic] 86-30587 ISBN 0-399-21387-2. First impression.

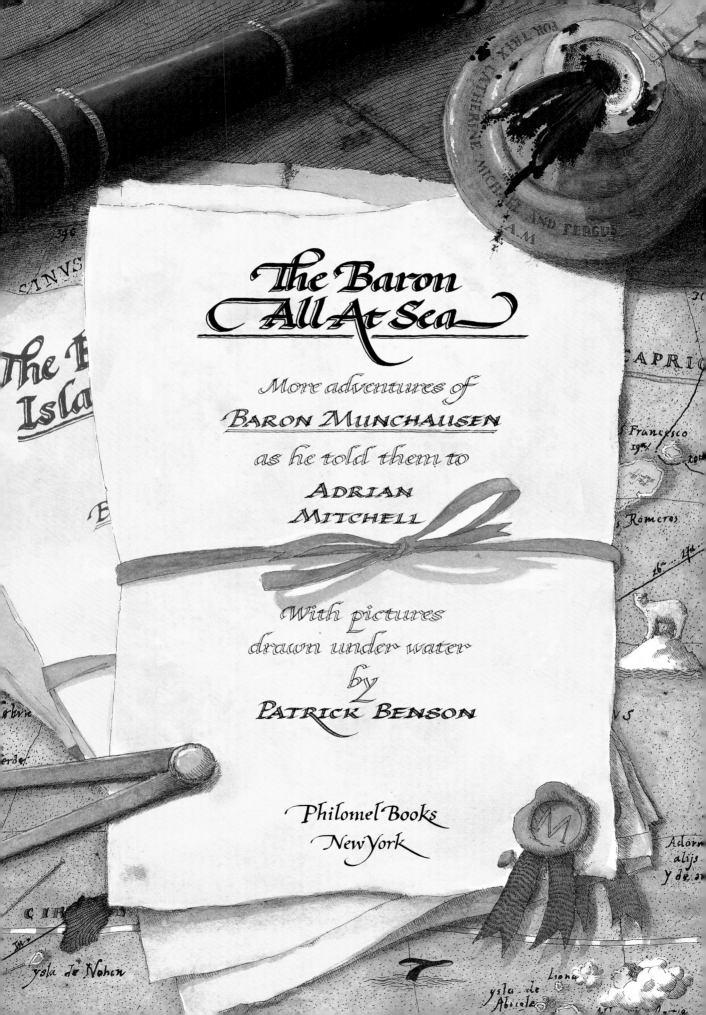

The Baron All At Sea

More adventures of

BARON MUNCHAUSEN

as he told them to

ADRIAN MITCHELL

With pictures
drawn under water
by

PATRICK BENSON

Philomel Books
New York

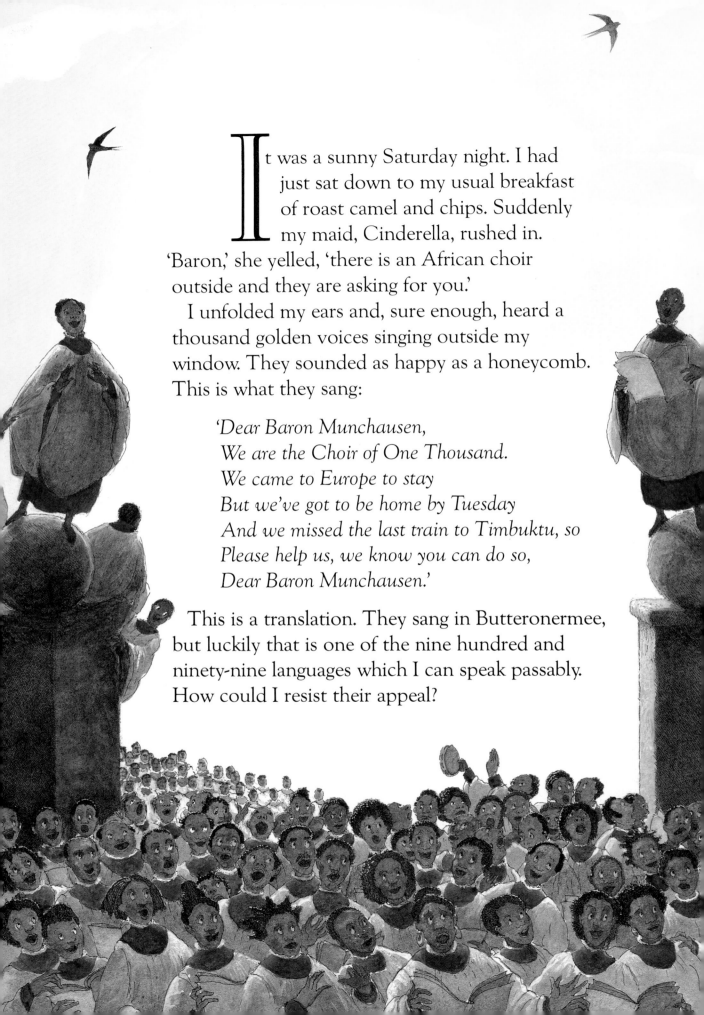

It was a sunny Saturday night. I had just sat down to my usual breakfast of roast camel and chips. Suddenly my maid, Cinderella, rushed in. 'Baron,' she yelled, 'there is an African choir outside and they are asking for you.'

I unfolded my ears and, sure enough, heard a thousand golden voices singing outside my window. They sounded as happy as a honeycomb. This is what they sang:

> 'Dear Baron Munchausen,
> We are the Choir of One Thousand.
> We came to Europe to stay
> But we've got to be home by Tuesday
> And we missed the last train to Timbuktu, so
> Please help us, we know you can do so,
> Dear Baron Munchausen.'

This is a translation. They sang in Butteronermee, but luckily that is one of the nine hundred and ninety-nine languages which I can speak passably. How could I resist their appeal?

Pausing only to shake their thousand hands,
I led the choir down to the Munchausen River
(which some call the Thames).

There we boarded my favorite vessel, the
Good Ship Taradiddle. As we cruised southwards
the Choir of One Thousand entertained me with
songs by Mozart, Beethoven and Munchausen.

Unluckily one of the Choir sang sharp. His
sharp note made a hole in the hull of the ship,
which sprang a leak. Water was pouring in fast.
All our pumps could not keep us from sinking.

I called to the Choir of One Thousand to jump
overboard and swim for it. They did so, with a
one thousandfold splash. Their hearts were heavy
at the loss of the ship, so unfortunately they all
sank to the bottom of the sea as fast as ferrets.

Meanwhile I had found the leak. The water
was roaring through a round hole about a yard
wide. I had one of my sudden ideas.

I sat down over the hole, plugging it with my
breeches. This prevented the ship from sinking,
although I found it rather cool.

Nobody was at the wheel, so the Taradiddle
steered herself. She was untrained in this art.
I found myself becoming colder and colder until
there was a sudden crash.

My ship had struck
against an ice-bound coast.
The shock was such that the
rudder snapped off and all the
masts jumped out of their sockets.

As for me, a waterspout lifted me clear of
the devastated ship and dropped me into a snow-
drift on the mainland. I fell upon my head, and was
thanking my lucky stars, when part of the snow
appeared to stand up and move towards me.

I realized that I was being stalked by that most
fearsome of creatures, the Giant Polar Bear. His
mouth opened in a snarl and I was able to count
at least seven rows of yellow teeth.

The animal obviously intended to enjoy a
Munchausen lunchausen. I am the mildest of men,
but I have done a little boxing. I prepared to
fell the bear with a right lower-cut to the gullet.

I made my move. My right foot slipped on the ice.
I fell upon my face. The monster picked me up by
the belt and began to carry me back to his icy lair.

I remembered my trusty penknife, (given me by
my 48 younger sisters and brothers). I drew
it from my pocket and opened its blade.
As I swung face downwards, I could
not see my opponent.

But I could hear his heartbeat. I lashed out towards that sound with my knife. My captor, with a terrible roar, dropped dead and dropped me at one and the same time.

His enormous roar woke several hundred of his fellow bears. They advanced on me. There was only one thing to do. I skinned the dead bear in less time than you would take to take off your socks. I wrapped myself in the bearskin just before the polar bears reached me.

They all came sniffing and smelling me. At once they accepted me as a brother Bruin and we became fast friends. I found that life as a bear was pleasant enough – a matter of growling, fishing, hugging, hibernating and scratching mostly.

But it was chilly work. One day I could not resist lighting a fire. My polar friends were amazed and delighted. They crowded around and warmed their paws at the flames.

Soon they became so warm that they took off their fur coats and lay down to bask in the heat. As soon as they were all sound asleep, I bundled up the coats and took my leave, as silent as a surgeon.

(At a later date I distributed these coats as presents among the many good people who write to me saying how much they enjoy my adventures.)

I was lucky enough to find an abandoned sledge
on the ice. But I had no dog to pull it for me.
At this very moment a huge wolf came loping by.

I called to him in my most commanding voice.
He stood stock still. By talking to him sternly,
I was able to harness him and make him pull my
sledge at a good pace towards the sea.

But wolves are untrustworthy beasts. The
moment I unharnessed him, he rushed at me.
By some instinct, I thrust my fist into his
open mouth.

For safety's sake, I pushed on and on, till my
arm was in up to my shoulder. But how could I get
out of this situation?

The wolf looked at me. I looked at the wolf.
We were face to face, but we did not see eye to eye.
If I withdrew my arm, this animal would bite my
head off. There was only one thing to do.

I pushed my arm further down into the wolf.
I laid hold of his tail, turning him inside out like a
glove, and flung him down on the snow. Then
I walked down to the sea and dived in.

The first water creature I encountered was
a Giant Sea-horse. These beasts cannot float or
move on the surface of the water. But they can
run with great speed along the sands at the
bottom of the sea.

I mounted my Giant Sea-horse and he carried
me over the sea-bed, driving fish in their millions
before him. We crossed one range of underwater
mountains at least as high as the Himalayas.

On the sides of these mountains stood many
fine trees, bearing ocean fruit such as lobsters,
crabs, oysters, mussels, etcetera. It was early
autumn and the first fruits were falling off their
branches, blown off by the currents
of the sea.

As we drew near the shore of Africa, I thought I saw another mountain. Then I realized that it was a pile of one thousand human bodies.

I had found the Choir of One Thousand lying on the ocean bed. They seemed to show some signs of life. My Sea-horse and I carried them to the surface in bundles of six. There I applied artificial respiration.

On the beach they began to breathe again. Pretty soon they were singing merrily as milk bottles:

'Thank you, Baron Munchausen,
For saving the Choir of One Thousand.
Otherwise we would be dead
Down upon the sea-bed.
Still we have to get to Timbuktu,
Please can we rely on you,
Dear Baron Munchausen?'

At that very moment Queen Mab came strolling along the beach. Now the Queen is an old friend of mine. When she heard of the plight of the Choir of One Thousand, she offered us the use of her chariot.

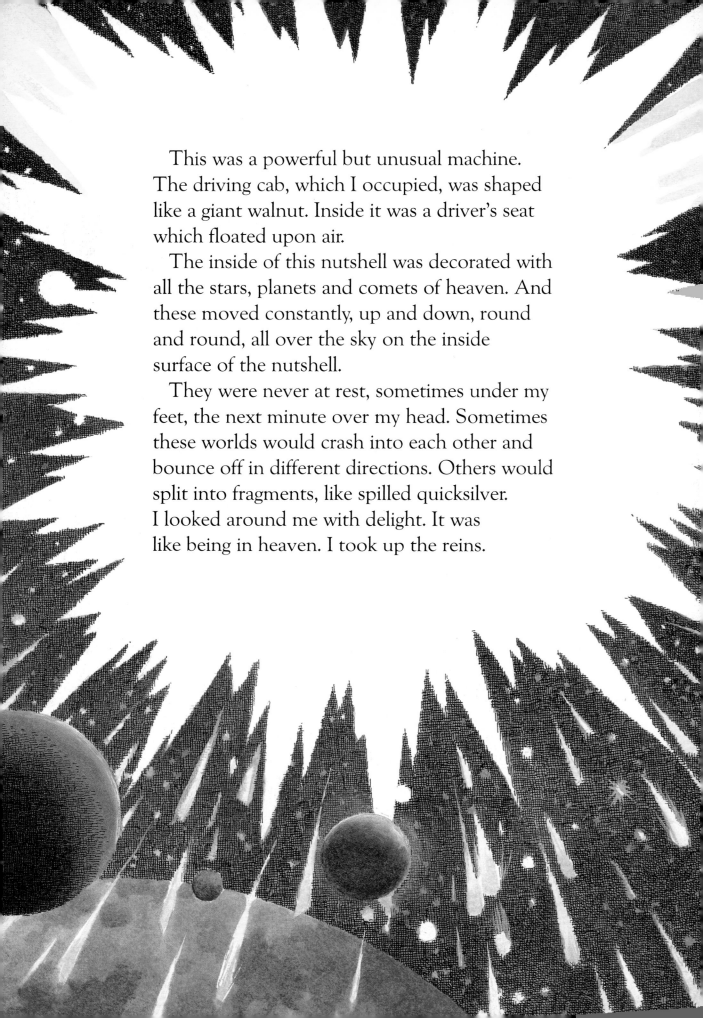

This was a powerful but unusual machine.
The driving cab, which I occupied, was shaped
like a giant walnut. Inside it was a driver's seat
which floated upon air.

The inside of this nutshell was decorated with
all the stars, planets and comets of heaven. And
these moved constantly, up and down, round
and round, all over the sky on the inside
surface of the nutshell.

They were never at rest, sometimes under my
feet, the next minute over my head. Sometimes
these worlds would crash into each other and
bounce off in different directions. Others would
split into fragments, like spilled quicksilver.
I looked around me with delight. It was
like being in heaven. I took up the reins.

But before we drive on, I should mention
the rest of my vehicle. Behind my nutshell was
drawn a forty-leven-storey hotel upon wheels, which
comfortably housed the Choir of One Thousand,
together with Queen Mab's servants.

This hotel had its own dining-room, of course,
together with a swimming pool and a concert hall
in which the Choir could rehearse. It may seem
unlikely that such a large building could travel
on wheels, but its weight was somewhat
relieved by a pair of large balloons.

The whole chariot was drawn by a team of nine bulls, harnessed in threes. These bold creatures could make astonishing journeys, sliding upon water, galloping over sand, cantering over mountains with great speed.

The bulls were harnessed in gold and ridden by nine coachmen – giant grasshoppers as large as monkeys. They sat upon the heads of the bulls and chirped loudly and continuously, much to my annoyance.

I cracked my whip and away we went, as smooth as smirking. In six jiffies I had delivered the Choir of One Thousand to their mother in Timbuktu. The city hourglass was striking midnight on Monday, so we were just in time.

Tuesday was the Choir's birthday. They had all been born on the same day, though in different years, of course. This may seem a strange coincidence, but it is as true as trapezes. We feasted upon their birthday cake, which had one thousand layers and thirty-three thousand candles

to represent their combined ages, more or less.

But as midnight struck, the chariot of Queen Mab vanished in a puff of stardust. How could I get home?

The simplest answer is often the best. I decided, with the help of the Choir of One Thousand, to construct a bridge between Africa and England.

The Tower of Babel was seven miles high – or so they say. But that was a mere pimple. The so-called Great Wall of China was nothing but a garden fence.

But my bridge was a bridge. It was like a stone rainbow in the sky. The base rose from the center of Africa. The other end seemed to stoop into north-west London.

There were some problems in building it. The arch was so high that gravitation was very low. At times the pull of other planets was such that the top stones tended to fall upwards.

When the bridge was finished, I decided to walk home, for the exercise. As I mounted the great arch, I heard a thousand voices below me singing:

> *'Dear Baron Munchausen,*
> *Goodbye from the Choir of One Thousand.'*

I would miss them in days to come.

The view from the center of the bridge was glorious. I looked down on the kingdoms and seas and islands below me. Africa seemed generally a tawny brownish color, burned up by the sun. Spain was more yellow, because of its fields of corn. France had a bright straw colour. But England was covered with a most beautiful green mantle.

I arrived home on Tuesday night, to be greeted by Cinderella. My roast camel was cold, so I left the hump.